The VISIT

CHAPTERS

by Meish Goldish
illustrated by Jeff Shelly

Harcourt

Orlando   Boston   Dallas   Chicago   San Diego

Visit *The Learning Site!*
www.harcourtschool.com

SHARING NEWS

Sean began to practice playing his clarinet. His mother entered the room.

"Is that a new song?" she asked.

Sean looked up. "Yes. I just got it. It's for the New Year Festival."

"Oh, I'm glad you reminded me," she replied. "I'd almost forgotten about it."

Sean made a funny face. "Mom, how could you forget! It's in two weeks. I want you and Dad to be there."

"We will, dear, we will. Only . . ." She stopped. Sean thought she looked puzzled.

"Only what?" Sean asked.

"I guess I forgot to tell you, Sean. Next week, your dad's uncle Robert is coming to visit us."

"From Scotland?" Sean asked.

"That's right," his mother said. "I'm surprised, too. We haven't been in close touch. Occasionally your dad sends him a holiday card. Your great uncle Robert is your grandpa's brother. He's never been here. Scotland and Wisconsin aren't neighbors. Scotland is pretty far away. It's a long trip."

"How long will he stay?" Sean asked.

"Until the day after New Year's Day," his mother replied. "Is it all right with you if we bring him to the festival?"

"Of course!" Sean cried.

"There's just one more thing," his mother added. "Uncle Robert was not happy that your dad's family left Scotland."

"Why did Dad leave?" Sean asked.

Sean's mother took out a photo album and shared pictures as she spoke.

"Your grandparents had a very small farm. It wasn't doing well. They tried irrigation. They tried everything," she said. "Nothing worked, and so Grandpa and Grandma came here. They wanted a big farm. When your father left Scotland, he was a young boy. He was younger than you are now."

"So Dad didn't decide to come here," Sean said.

"You're right," his mother said. "Grandpa and Grandma decided to leave. Robert was unhappy that they moved so far away. He still is unhappy about it."

"Does he know we're happy here in Wisconsin?" Sean asked.

"Oh, yes," his mother said. "He's glad about that. He's also very proud of Scotland—Scottish foods, Scottish music, the Scottish language."

Sean interrupted, "Does Uncle Robert speak English?"

"Oh, yes!" his mother laughed. "Don't worry. You won't need an interpreter."

Sean smiled. "I'm glad he's coming, Mom."

5

Meeting the Guest

Uncle Robert sat down. This was his first American breakfast. Sean's mother gave him a bowl of oatmeal. "This porridge looks very appetizing indeed. Thank you, lassie," he said. "Porridge, or oatmeal, is a Scottish dish. Did you know that, laddie?" he asked Sean.

Sean shook his head. "No."

"In Scotland, we even make crackers with oatmeal!" Robert added.

"They're called oatcakes," Sean's dad said.

Robert winked. "I'm glad you remember that. You used to love oatcakes."

After breakfast, Sean's mother had an idea. "Sean, why don't you take Uncle Robert for a walk? He's never seen our town."

Sean and his uncle went outside and began walking.

"I'm glad I brought my warmest coat," Uncle Robert said. "Your winters seem to be a wee bit cold. We have cold days in Scotland, too, but not this cold."

Sean said, smiling, "I'm glad you came at this time of year. You'll be able to hear me play in my band next week. We're playing in the New Year Festival."

"What instrument do you play?" Uncle Robert asked.

"Clarinet," Sean answered.

Uncle Robert looked at him. "Not the bagpipes?"

"No, Uncle Robert. I play the clarinet. I like it."

They turned the corner. "There's my school," said Sean. "That's where the festival will be."

Uncle Robert seemed not to hear. He asked, "How could you not play the bagpipes, laddie? They're the best instrument in all of music. There is no equivalent."

"Uncle Robert, I don't think I know anyone who plays the bagpipes."

"Your grandfather played them, Sean. Did you know that?" asked Uncle Robert.

Sean shook his head.

"Please tell me more about Grandpa," Sean said. "I don't remember him very well."

"Your grandpa was the best bagpipe player in our village," Uncle Robert explained. "His playing could just overwhelm you! He played at every festival." He stopped for a minute. "Sean, why don't you learn to play the bagpipes?" he asked. "Then you can play in honor of your grandpa and Scotland."

Sean saw how serious Uncle Robert was.

"I wish I could," Sean said. "I don't know who could teach me, and I don't own any bagpipes."

They looked in the music store. Sean had no idea what Uncle Robert was planning.

Sean's parents were good friends with Mr. and Mrs. Stein. Mr. Stein was the music teacher at Sean's school. One night, the Steins came over for dinner and to meet Uncle Robert.

"Has your uncle got you singing 'Auld Lang Syne' yet?" Mr. Stein asked Sean.

"Old lang sign?" Sean asked.

"'Auld Lang Syne,'" Mr. Stein repeated. "It's a Scottish song. The title means 'old times.' People sing it on New Year's Eve."

Mr. Stein began to sing. "Should old acquaintance be forgot, and never brought to mind . . ."

"I know that song!" Sean cried.

Mr. Stein turned to Uncle Robert. "Will you be coming to the New Year Festival? You'll get to hear Sean play the clarinet."

"I wouldn't miss it! I just wish someone in the family would carry on the tradition of playing the bagpipes," said Uncle Robert.

Several days later, the whole family greatly enjoyed the New Year Festival—especially the clarinet playing.

A few days after Uncle Robert left, a large box arrived for Sean. A note inside the box read, "Please speak with Mr. Stein, your music teacher. It's all arranged. Love, Great Uncle Robert." In the box were a set of bagpipes, another pipe instrument, and a book.

Sean took the whole box to school. He found his teacher in the band room. "Mr. Stein, I know this sounds funny, but please don't laugh hysterically. Do you think that by next year's concert I could learn to play a song on the bagpipes? Uncle Robert is talking about coming back next year, and I'd love to surprise him."

Mr. Stein took a deep breath. "The bagpipe is a very difficult instrument to learn. Usually it takes several years. However, a good clarinet player like you might be able to do it."

"It would have to be a simple song," Mr. Stein explained. "A song with no more than six or seven notes. 'Auld Lang Syne' would be perfect."

After school, Mr. Stein showed Sean how to play the chanter, a practice pipe for beginners.

"Blow through the reed. It is like the clarinet," he explained. It took several tries for Sean to get a good sound out of the pipe. Finally, he found the right way.

Next, Mr. Stein showed Sean how to cover the pipe holes with his fingers. As he covered and uncovered the holes, the sound came out.

"It's a lot like playing the clarinet!" Sean cried.

Mr. Stein smiled. He was glad that the chanter did not overwhelm his student.

For several months, Sean played the chanter. He practiced every day. Mr. Stein came to Sean's house each week. He helped him practice. Week by week, Sean's playing improved.

At last, Mr. Stein thought Sean was ready to try the bagpipes. It was much more difficult than Sean had expected. He had to learn how to use his arm to pump the bag full of air. He had to learn to control the flow of air to the pipes. At the same time, he had to blow into the reed and use his fingers to play the notes!

The New Year Festival was just a few months away. Would Sean be able to play well by then?

The Concert

Uncle Robert had arrived from Scotland just two days before. Sean's father joked with him that maybe he would soon decide to leave Scotland, too.

"Have you been playing the bagpipes?" was his first question to Sean.

Sean grinned and said, "I'm trying, Uncle Robert, I really am, but it's a very difficult instrument."

The night of the New Year Festival finally came. All the way to school, Sean played "Auld Lang Syne" in his head. Standing backstage, he felt very, very nervous.

As the program began, he calmed down. Sean and the rest of the school band played all their songs well.

At the end of the evening, Mr. Stein thanked everyone who played and the people who came to listen.

Then he said, "Our concert isn't over just yet. As a final treat at this New Year Festival, I give you Sean Douglas."

Sean walked to center stage, with his bagpipes. He took a deep breath. "Tonight, I will welcome in the New Year with an old Scottish song."

"I want to thank Mr. Stein, who taught me how to play the bagpipes. I also want to thank my great uncle Robert, who asked me to do this. This song is in memory of my grandfather, one of the finest pipers in all of Scotland."

The room grew very quiet. Sean began to play, and the notes came out sweetly. He pressed the air bag and covered the holes skillfully.

The audience stood up. They began to sing! Sean could see Uncle Robert hugging his father and mother. They swayed to the music.

"To the good old days!" Uncle Robert cried proudly. "For auld lang syne!"